# Top 10 Pitchers

Chris W. Sehnert

ABDO & Daughters
Publishing

Published by Abdo & Daughters, 4940 Viking Drive, Suite 622, Edina, Minnesota 55435.

Copyright © 1997 by Abdo Consulting Group, Inc., Pentagon Tower, P.O. Box 36036, Minneapolis, Minnesota 55435 USA.  International copyrights reserved in all countries. No part of this book may be reproduced in any form without written permission from the publisher.

Printed in the United States.

Cover and Interior Photo credits: Allsports Photos
Wide World Photos
Bettmann Photos
Sports Illustrated

Edited by Paul Joseph

### Library of Congress Cataloging-in-Publication Data

Sehnert, Chris W.
    Top 10 Pitchers / Chris W. Sehnert.
    p.    cm. -- (Top 10 Champions)
    Includes index.
    Summary:  Profiles the lives and careers of Cy Young, Greg Maddux, Christy Mathewson, Whitey Ford, Sandy Koufax, Bob Gibson, Jim Palmer, Catfish Hunter, Nolan Ryan, and Fernando Valenzuela.
    ISBN 1-56239-798-2
    1. Pitchers (Baseball)--United States--Biography--Juvenile literature. 2. Pitchers (Baseball)--Rating of--United States--Juvenile literature. [1. Baseball players.] I. Title. II. Series: Sehnert, Chris W.  Top 10 champions
    GV865.A1S386    1997
    796.357'22'092273--dc21                                    97-15846
    [B]                                                                        CIP
                                                                                AC

# Table of Contents

# Cy Young

The center of a diamond is a special place. It is where light is gathered from all directions before being refracted into a brilliant spectrum of color. At the center of a baseball diamond is the pitcher's mound, where many of the most colorful *Champions* have climbed "The Hill" on their way into sports history. Often the destiny of a baseball team is placed squarely on the pitcher's shoulders. In Major League Baseball, nobody has spent more time at the center of the diamond than a pitcher who became commonly known as "Cyclone!"

His name was Denton True Young, but virtually everyone remembers him as "Cy." In 22 major league seasons, beginning in 1890, Cy Young compiled the greatest pitching record in the history of the game. With over 7,000 innings of major league mound-work, no other pitcher has ever approached his incredible durability or consistency. At a position where 300 wins places a player among the game's all-time elite, Cy Young was victorious 511 times! In the National League (NL), he was a champion with the Cleveland Spiders. Then in 1903, he led the American League's Boston Pilgrims to the first World Championship of the modern baseball era. Today, at the end of every season, one outstanding pitcher from each league is awarded a trophy bearing the name of Cy Young.

Denton True Young was born on a farm near Gilmore, Ohio, in 1867. Just after his second birthday, a ballclub from the southern part of his home state became the first to declare themselves as professional. Two years later, the Cincinnati Red Stockings moved to Boston, Massachusetts, and became members of the National Association. Major League Baseball had begun, and from that day forward young Americans like Dent Young would begin dreaming of a career in the big leagues.

Farming prior to the days of modern machinery and motorized tractors was a very difficult task, and Denton grew strong from his chores. In these early days of baseball, when pitchers threw underhand while standing in a flat box 45 feet from home plate, Denton became a burly third-baseman where his powerful arm was more suited to the task. When the overhand pitch was legalized in 1884, the Cyclone began to twirl.

In 1890, Cy Young had won 15 games for a minor-league team in Canton, Ohio, when his contract was purchased by the Cleveland Spiders. He threw a three-hitter in his major league debut, and the next season his 27 wins began a nine-year streak with 20 or more victories per year. By 1892, the NL had successfully monopolized Major League Baseball, and post-season play consisted of a battle between the league's first and second-place finishers. The Spiders

competed in three of these so-called Temple-Cups, and with the help of Cy's three victories, defeated the Baltimore Orioles in 1895 to become World Champions.

The American League (AL) became the NL's chief rival in 1901. By offering higher wages to its players, the new league quickly gathered up many of the NL's greatest stars. Included among them was Cy Young, who led the AL in wins for three-straight seasons. By 1903, the AL declared itself the equal of its more established counterpart, and the modern baseball era was underway. That season, Cy Young's Boston Pilgrims won the AL Pennant and defeated the Pittsburgh Pirates in the first World Series of the Twentieth Century!

**PROFILE:**
Cy Young
Born: March 29, 1867
Died: November 4, 1955
Height: 6' 2"
Weight: 210 pounds
Position: Pitcher
Teams: Cleveland Spiders (1890-1898), St. Louis Cardinals (1899-1900), Boston Pilgrims (1901-1908), Cleveland Indians (1909-1911), Boston Braves (1911)

## CHAMPIONSHIP SEASONS

Cy Young as a
Cleveland Spider.

1895
**Temple Cup**
Cleveland Spiders (4) vs.
Baltimore Orioles (1)

1903
**World Series**
Boston Pilgrims (5) vs.
Pittsburgh Pirates (3)

# YESTERDAY

Baseball has gone through comparatively few rule changes since its development in the 1840s. Back then, Alexander Cartwright and the New York Knickerbockers ballclub put their version of the game on paper. They established that "base ball" was to be played on a diamond with 90 foot baselines, the three strikes and you're out rule, and three outs per half-inning of play. These and other Knickerbocker guidelines were adopted by the National Association when it became baseball's first professional league in 1871.

Perhaps the most profound variations in the game have surrounded the duel between pitcher and batter. Originally, the pitcher was allowed to have a running windup within a six-foot box before hurling the ball in a strictly underhand motion. As batters began to gain the upper-hand, the side-arm delivery was allowed, which in turn led to the development of the first curve-ball. Eventually, the windup was restricted to begin from a standing position 45 feet from home-plate, and the overhand delivery was accepted.

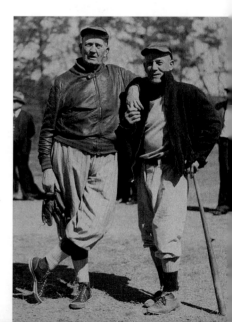

*Cy Young (L) with teammate.*

# AND TODAY

In the early 1890s, fireballing NL hurlers like Cy Young and Amos Rusie were becoming down right dangerous. The league responded by moving the pitcher's box back to its present distance of 60-feet, 6-inches, in 1893. With the inception of baseball's modern era in 1903, the pitcher's box was transformed into a mound, rising 15 inches above the playing surface.

To this day, baseball's rule-makers continue to make subtle adjustments to ensure even-handedness in the relationship between pitcher and batter. The mound was lowered to its present height of 10 inches above home-plate after the 1968 season, which became known as "The Year of the Pitcher." In the 1990s, with major league sluggers clouting home runs in record numbers, there have been discussions of raising the mound back up!

*Cy Young playing in an old-timers game.*

# *C*YCLONE'S ENDLESS REIGN

Cy Young led the NL in shutout victories four times in the nineteenth century, and tossed the first of his three no-hitters in 1897. Four years later, he became the first AL pitcher to complete a Triple Crown (leading the league in wins, earned run average, and strikeouts). In 1904, his second no-hitter came in the form of a perfect game (allowing no baserunners). He completed the season by leading the AL in shutouts for the third time in four years. At the age of 41, the remarkable Cy Young fired his third no-hitter, and rounded off the last of his record 15 20-win seasons!

# Christy
# Mathewson

Baseball has been known as America's national pastime since the country was reunited following the Civil War. For more than a century, the major leagues have represented the game's finest talent, but not necessarily the most upstanding individuals. Ballplayers are not often thought of in terms of their good-deeds, but for a feisty competitiveness and overwhelming desire to win. The rivalries that result from competition can lead to fierce battles-of-will and damage a person's reputation. Yet, there are those who have combined their passion for victory with character in the face of combat. These were the distinguishing qualities of a true American hero named Christy Mathewson.

The National League is known as baseball's "Senior Circuit." It was established in 1876, when it took over for the poorly organized National Association. Four years later the person destined to become the new league's most dominant pitcher was born in the small town of Factoryville, Pennsylvania.

After compiling the greatest pitching record in the history of the NL, Christy Mathewson would join America's fighting forces on the Western Front of World War I. Prior to arriving in the Senior Circuit, "Matty" was a scholar and All-American football player at Bucknell University!

Christopher Mathewson was the oldest of Gilbert and Minerva Mathewson's six children. Gilbert helped his father construct the family's log cabin, before joining the Union forces in the Civil War. When the conflict ended he returned to Factoryville, where he married Minerva

Capwell. Together they built a family farm of their own, and raised their children under the strict code of the Baptist religious faith. Minerva wanted for her eldest son to become a preacher. Young Christy had other ideas, but he would forever keep his vow to her never to play baseball on Sunday.

Aside from religion, the Mathewson's encouraged their children to educate themselves in order to avoid a destiny in the local coal mines. Christy's grandmother was a teacher and founded the Keystone Academy, where he prepared himself for college. He took his studies seriously, and also excelled on the school's football, basketball, and baseball teams. In his spare time, Christy studied the mechanics of the throwing motion. He spent hours tossing rocks until he had developed incredible accuracy as well as a very powerful arm.

Christy began playing semi-professional baseball at the age of 15. By the time he entered Bucknell University in the fall of 1898, he had already spent three summers as a minor-league hurler. As a college student he was elected Class President, before dropping out after his junior year to pursue his record-setting career in the big leagues.

On April 26, 1901, Christy Mathewson recorded the first of his 373 NL victories. Four years later he would shutout the AL's powerful Philadelphia Athletics three-straight times in leading the New York Giants to the second World Championship of baseball's modern era. The handsome All-American became Major League Baseball's first superstar attraction, drawing millions of fans to the ballpark to partake in his performances, which never took place on Sunday.

**PROFILE:**
Christy Mathewson
Born: August 12, 1880
Died: November 7, 1925
Height: 6' 1"
Weight: 195 pounds
Position: Pitcher
Throws: Right
Teams: New York Giants (1900-1916), Cincinnati Reds (1916)

## CHAMPIONSHIP

### SEASONS

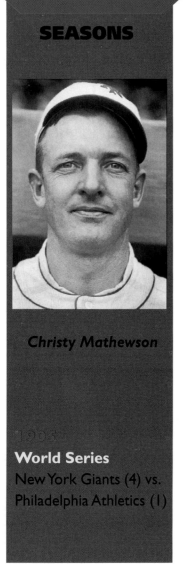

*Christy Mathewson*

1905

**World Series**
New York Giants (4) vs.
Philadelphia Athletics (1)

## BIG SIX AND LITTLE NAPOLEON

Christy Mathewson became known as "Big Six" when New York sportswriters likened his fastball's velocity to that of a local fire engine. In 1902, however, Christy began to struggle on the mound, and management seriously considered converting him into a shortstop. Later that season, John McGraw became the Giants' new manager and proclaimed the experiment to move Matty as "sheer insanity."

McGraw would remain as New York's field-boss for 31 seasons and came to be known as "Little Napoleon" for his tyrannical temper. His bitter war with the American League, where he managed the Baltimore Orioles before jumping to the Giants, caused the cancellation of the 1904 World Series. The next season, New York won the NL Pennant for the second straight time and defeated the Philadelphia Athletics in the Fall Classic, as post-season play was resumed.

**Christy Mathewson with the New York Giants.**

# FREAK-BALL

The consummate control pitcher, Matty had a blazing fastball and an equally effective curve-ball. His most devastating delivery, however, was something he liked to call his "freak-ball." The pitch had a backwards breaking-motion to that of a normal curve and was later labeled the "fadeaway" for its effect on left-handed batters. Christy Mathewson employed his three-pitch arsenal to win 373 ballgames, a NL record later tied by Grover Cleveland "Pete" Alexander. Matty also won two NL Triple Crowns and is baseball's all-time leader with four shutouts and ten complete games in the Fall Classic.

Carl Hubbell came to the New York Giants in 1928. He was discovered by John McGraw who noticed that the left-hander had a backward breaking-ball that resembled Matty's famous fadeaway. "King Carl" called his pitch the "screw-ball," but was banned from using it while in the Detroit Tigers' minor-league system. In New York, Carl Hubbell would pitch 16 seasons, lead the Giants to the 1933 World Championship, and later join Christy Mathewson in the Baseball Hall of Fame.

# AMERICAN HEROISM

In 1916, Christy Mathewson left the New York Giants to become a player-manager for the Cincinnati Reds. He pitched in only one game for the Reds and recorded his final victory. When America became involved in World War I, Christy enlisted in the armed services and was sent to the Western Front. While serving as a Captain in the Army's gas-and-flame division he was exposed to poison gas, which caused him to suffer pulmonary tuberculosis. Christy Mathewson died at the age of 45, and was elected to the Hall of Fame's inaugural class in 1936, along with Babe Ruth, Honus Wagner, Ty Cobb, and Walter Johnson.

# Whitey
# Ford

Confidence is a state of assurance in one's own abilities. Without it, a pitcher is doomed to failure before he reaches the mound. It may be instilled through success, bolstered by the support of others, or gained through sheer strength of will. Whatever the means, few pitchers have carried themselves with more confidence than Whitey Ford.

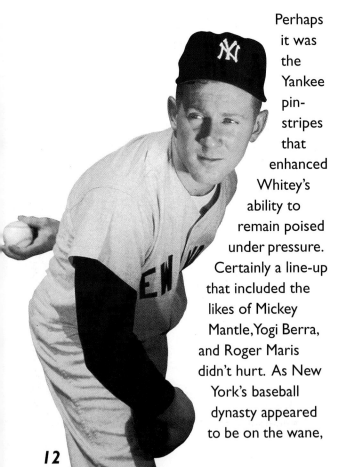

Perhaps it was the Yankee pin-stripes that enhanced Whitey's ability to remain poised under pressure. Certainly a line-up that included the likes of Mickey Mantle, Yogi Berra, and Roger Maris didn't hurt. As New York's baseball dynasty appeared to be on the wane,

however, manager Casey Stengle was quick to point out the value of the cocky little left-hander who won more World Series contests than any man in history. "Whitey used to stick out his chest and walk out to the mound against any of those big pitchers," Casey re-marked. "They talk about the fall of the Yankees. Well, the Yankees would have fallen a lot sooner if it wasn't for my banty rooster."

Edwin Charles Ford was born in midtown Manhattan. Before long, the little bundle whose eyelashes were as blonde as the hair on his head would gain his nickname for life. Whitey's father James was a bartender, and his mother's name was Edith. The family moved to the Astoria section of Queens, New York, when he was still a child. As a five-foot, four-inch teenager, Whitey played baseball for the Thirty-fourth Avenue Boys Club of Astoria. Soon they would become the most successful sandlot team in the neighborhood.

The high school nearest Whitey's childhood home was William Cullen Bryant in Long Island City.

Noting there was no baseball team at that institution, Whitey transferred to the Manhattan High School of Aviation Trades. For two hours each day he would ride the subway to and from school in order to have a place to show off his talents. Two months after his graduation, he was invited to tryout for the New York Yankees.

Whitey spent three seasons in the Yankees' minor-league system, where he exuded the confidence of a wily veteran. "Put me in," he demanded of the Binghamton Triplets' manager whenever a lesser teammate got into a jam. "I can stop these guys." With the New York ballclub battling for the 1949 American League Championship, Whitey expressed his frustration over not being called to "The Show." "I've been reading in the papers that Stengel is looking all over the country for a pitcher that can win the pennant for him," he complained. "Why don't he look in Binghamton?" The next season, the great Yankee manager did just that.

On July 1, 1950, Whitey Ford made his debut in Yankee pinstripes. He won nine consecutive starting assignments that season, the last of which was a pennant-clinching victory over the Detroit Tigers.

His triumph over Philadelphia's "Whiz Kids" finished off New York's four game sweep of the Fall Classic. Whitey would spend the next two seasons as a private in the Army signal corps during the Korean War.

When he returned to New York's lineup in 1953, Whitey rekindled a career that would result in the highest winning percentage of any twentieth century pitcher. Along the way, he set numerous World Series records including his 33 consecutive scoreless-innings streak, which broke a 45 year old mark formerly held by Babe Ruth. Mickey Mantle, who broke a number of Babe's Fall Classic records himself, knew exactly what made his teammate so successful. "Off the field Whitey was as smooth as butter," the Mick told reporters. "Stick a baseball in his hand, and he became the most arrogant guy in the world."

**PROFILE**:
Whitey Ford
Born: October 21, 1928
Height: 5' 10"
Weight: 181 pounds
Position: Pitcher
Throws: Left
Teams: New York Yankees (1950, 1953-1967)

## CHAMPIONSHIP

### SEASONS

1950

**World Series**

New York Yankees (4) vs.
Philadelphia Phillies (0)

1953

**World Series**

New York Yankees (4) vs.
Brooklyn Dodgers (2)

1956

**World Series**

New York Yankees (4) vs.
Brooklyn Dodgers (3)

1958

**World Series**

New York Yankees (4) vs.
Milwaukee Braves (3)

1961

**World Series**

New York Yankees (4) vs.
Cincinnati Reds (1)

1962

**World Series**

New York Yankees (4) vs.
San Francisco Giants (3)

# FOR THE RECORD

Whitey Ford was a member of 11 American League Championship teams. In his 22 World Series games that he started, Whitey pitched 146 innings, struck out 94 batters, and was the winning pitcher 10 times! Each one of those marks represents a World Series record for mound-men.

Whitey's most impressive Fall Classic feat was his 33 consecutive scoreless-innings streak. It began with back-to-back shutouts over the Pittsburgh Pirates in the 1960 World Series. Whitey's streak continued in 1961, with 14 more innings of scoreless work and ended in Game 1 of the 1962 Fall Classic. The former record holder was also a former Yankee. Babe Ruth's 29 innings of scoreless World Series work (1916-1918) was accomplished as a pitcher for the Boston Red Sox, however.

During the regular season, Whitey led the American League in shutouts, earned run average, and innings-pitched two times each. He led the league in wins three times, and was the 1961 Cy Young Award winner. That season, Whitey's accomplishments were over shadowed by teammate Roger Maris, whose 61 home runs broke another one of the Babe's long standing records!

*Whitey Ford*

# STICKY SITUATION

Late in his career, Whitey was often suspected of skullduggery on the mound and was later proven to have "doctored" baseballs. Using the sharp edge of his wedding ring, he would apply a nick in the horse-hide, which gave him the grip he needed to throw an un-hittable sinker.

In a related incident, Whitey would apply a sticky resin to his fingertips, which he stored in a roll-on deodorant bottle. When Yogi Berra pilfered his teammate's locker in search of personal-hygiene, his arms became cemented to his sides! The Yankee's trainer had to trim the under-arm hair of the humorous Hall-of-Fame catcher in order to set him free.

*Ford with the NY Yankees.*

*Whitey Ford winding up.*

*Whitey Ford loved the game of baseball.*

15

# Sandy
# Koufax

**F**anning a flame will cause a fire to burn with more fury. However, the most brilliant blazes burn only briefly before bowing to the forces of nature. In the history of Major League Baseball, few have burned more brightly than a flame-throwing left-hander named Sandy Koufax. In an all too brief career, Sandy fanned more opposing batters per game than any pitcher who preceded him. On the other hand, maybe it was the wind from all of those strikeouts that caused his arm to burn itself out!

He was born Sanford Braun in the borough of Brooklyn, New York. Before he reached the age of three, his mother Evelyn would remarry to Irving Koufax and pass the new name on to her child. Irving was an attorney who moved the family to Rockville Centre, Long Island, before returning to Brooklyn when Sandy was 14. There, the lanky long-armed teenager grew up playing basketball at local Jewish community clubs and school yards.

Baseball was merely a way for Sandy to stay occupied when the basketball season had ended. At Lafayette High School, he was a light-hitting first baseman, but starred on the hard-court. He received a basketball scholarship from the University of Cincinnati, where he planned to become an architect. "The last thing that entered my mind was becoming a professional athlete," he remembers. There was no way of knowing that in a short time Sandy Koufax would become the youngest player ever to be elected into the Baseball Hall of Fame.

Sandy began pitching for a summer sandlot team while he was still in high school. When he learned his college baseball team would be traveling to New Orleans, he decided to tryout. In 32 innings of mound-work, he fanned 51 batters, drawing the attention of

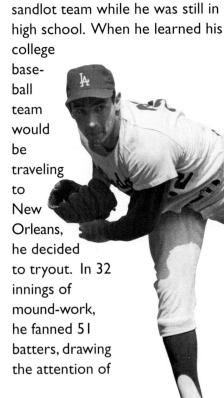

major league scouts from across the country. Before completing his sophomore season, the fire-balling 19 year old was signed to a contract with the Brooklyn Dodgers.

While the Dodgers won their first World Championship in Sandy's rookie season, his own contribution was slight. Through his first six seasons he showed flashes of brilliance, while struggling to gain control over his blazing fastball. In 1959, after the team had moved to Los Angeles, California, he struck-out 18 San Francisco Giants in one game, tying a major league record held by "Rapid" Robert Feller. Sandy made his first World Series appearance that season, losing a 1-0 decision before the Dodgers went on to win a second World Championship.

Dissatisfied with his performance in 1960, Sandy considered giving up the game to sell lighting fixtures. Instead he lit up the National League, opening the 1961 season with six consecutive complete-game victories and closing it by breaking Christy Mathewson's record for strikeouts in a season. The next year he threw the first of a record four no-hit ballgames and tied his own record with another 18-strikeout performance.

By the age of 26, Sandy Koufax was the hottest pitcher in all of baseball. Over the next five seasons, he won five National League ERA titles, three Triple Crowns for pitching, three Cy Young Awards, and the league's MVP honor. He led the Dodgers to another pair of World Championships, fanned 15 New York Yankees in one game, and continued to hold the lowest ERA in the history of the Fall Classic.

Sandy Koufax had yet to reach 31 years of age when the fire went out. Refusing to endure the scorching pain in his arthritic elbow any longer, he retired after the 1966 season. He went out in a blaze of glory, setting a National League record for left-handers with 27 wins in his final season. The memory of his fastball's heat continues to warm the hearts of baseball fans everywhere.

**PROFILE:**
Sandy Koufax
Born: December 30, 1935
Height: 6' 2"
Weight: 210 pounds
Position: Pitcher
Throws: Left
Teams: Brooklyn Dodgers (1955-1957), Los Angeles Dodgers (1958-1966)

## CHAMPIONSHIP
### SEASONS

**1955**

**World Series**
Brooklyn Dodgers (4) vs.
New York Yankees (3)

**1959**

**World Series**
Los Angeles Dodgers (4)
vs. Chicago White Sox (2)

**1963**

**World Series**
Los Angeles Dodgers (4)
vs. New York Yankees (0)

**1965**

**World Series**
Los Angeles Dodgers (4)
vs. Minnesota Twins (3)

# SOUTHPAWS

In a traditional baseball stadium, the pitching mound faces west. This accounts for the shadows that overtake home-plate during late afternoon ballgames. Because of this arrangement, the arm of a left-handed pitcher is on the south-side of his body. Thus the term "southpaw," which has come to describe any left-handed person, has its origins in baseball.

Sandy Koufax is considered by many to have been the greatest southpaw pitcher in the history of baseball. His competition for such high status includes Robert "Lefty" Grove and Steve "Lefty" Carlton.

Lefty Grove was the American League Most Valuable Player (MVP) in 1931, after winning his second-consecutive pitching Triple Crown and leading the Philadelphia Athletics to their third-straight AL Pennant. His 31 victories that season are more than any other 20th Century southpaw!

Lefty Carlton is baseball's all-time left-handed strikeout leader. He tied Sandy's modern-day National League record with 27 wins, during his Triple Crown season of 1972. Three years earlier, Carlton surpassed another of Koufax's National League marks with 19 strikeouts in a single game. He also won four Cy Young Awards and led the Philadelphia Phillies to their only World Championship in 1980.

# SANDY'S STRIKEOUTS

Sandy's record of 382 strikeouts in 1965 continues to rank as the most by any southpaw in a single-season. Right-hander Nolan Ryan currently holds the modern day record with 383 strikeouts in 1973. Nolan also broke Sandy's all-time record of four no-hit performances.

*Sandy Koufax pitching for the Dodgers.*

*Sandy's classic wind up.*

19

# Bob
# Gibson

Pitchers hold the key to success for every baseball team. The statement "Good pitching defeats good hitting," is one of the game's oldest adages. It was never more true than in 1968, when Bob Gibson reached the peak of his career in a season remembered as "The Year of the Pitcher!"

In baseball's early years, the game was played base-to-base with the bunt, stolen base, and hit-and-run plays serving as primary offensive strategies. The ball itself was rarely replaced during the course of a game and became heavy with dirt and slime before the contest was over.

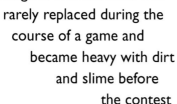

In this "Dead-Ball Era," pitchers frequently surrendered fewer than two runs per game. It came to a fatal conclusion in 1919, when a pitch from fireballing Carl Mays struck Rex Chapman in the head. The next season, Babe Ruth slammed 54 brand-new, cork-centered baseball's out of the park, nearly doubling his own previous single-season record.

In 1935, Babe hit the last of his 714 career home runs, and a pitcher named Robert Louis Gibson was born in the town of Omaha, Nebraska. Young Bob would reach 11 years of age before African-American ballplayers were finally allowed to compete in the major leagues. After leading the St. Louis Cardinals to a pair of World Championships, Bob Gibson posted the National League's finest single-season pitching performance since the masterful Mordecai "Three-Finger" Brown's in 1906.

Bob's 13 shutout victories in 1968 helped bring St. Louis their third National League Pennant in five

seasons. The Cardinals were defeated in a seven game World Series by the Detroit Tigers, whose staff-ace Denny McLain completed a historic season of his own. Baseball had come full circle, as deadball returned in "The Year of the Pitcher."

Bob Gibson was the seventh child of Pack and Victoria Gibson. His father, who was a mill worker, died a month before Bob's birth. Victoria went to work in a laundry to support her large family, and her youngest son soon began fighting for his own life. Bob was a sickly child whose afflictions included rickets, asthma, and a rheumatic heart condition. At the age of three, he spent several months in a hospital while suffering complications from pneumonia.

Recovering from his childhood ailments, Bob took an interest in sports. His older brother Leroy was an athletic director for the local YMCA and encouraged him to excel. At Omaha Technical High School, Bob participated in the high-jump for track, was a catcher on the baseball team, and a star on the basketball court. He received a basketball scholarship from

Creighton University where he majored in sociology and was a hard-hitting shortstop for the baseball team.

In 1957, a scout from the St. Louis Cardinals spotted Bob hurling in a semi-professional league. The scout noted: "He could throw the ball through the side of a barn, if he could only hit the barn," Bob was signed to a contract and converted into a full-time pitcher. Five years later, Bob would lead the National League in shutout victories for the first of four times in his career. In "The Year of the Pitcher," Bob Gibson was the league's MVP and Cy Young Award winner. His 1.12 ERA that season beckoned the days of Mordecai Brown, Christy Mathewson and the "Dead-Ball Era."

**_PROFILE_:**
Bob Gibson
Born: November 9, 1935
Height: 6' 2"
Weight: 195 pounds
Position: Pitcher
Throws: Right
Teams: St. Louis Cardinals (1959-1975)

## CHAMPIONSHIP
### SEASONS

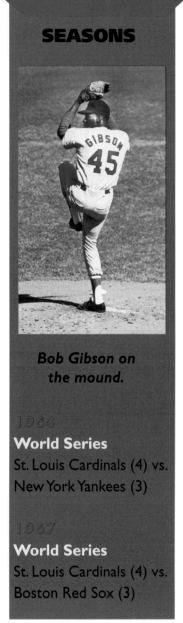

*Bob Gibson on
the mound.*

1964

**World Series**
St. Louis Cardinals (4) vs.
New York Yankees (3)

1967

**World Series**
St. Louis Cardinals (4) vs.
Boston Red Sox (3)

# ERA
# OF ERA'S

Earned Run Average (ERA) is the most accurate statistic for determining a pitcher's effectiveness. It calculates the number of runs allowed per nine innings, discounting those that score through no fault of the person on the mound. It is also an excellent means of tracking the way the game has been played through the ages.

Tim Keefe (0.86 ERA in 1880) and Dutch Leonard (0.96 ERA in 1914) are the only major league pitchers who have allowed less than one run per game over an entire season. Mordecai "Three Finger" Brown (1.04 ERA in 1906) ranks third on the list followed by Bob Gibson (1.12 ERA in 1968). "Gibby" is the only member of the four all-time leaders whose career season included more than 300 innings of mound-work!

*Bob Gibson
delivers a pitch.*

# DEAD-BALL

In the 1960s, the St. Louis Cardinals won baseball games the old-fashioned way. They were consistently among the top of the league in hits, while at the bottom of the list for home runs. Their lead-off batter was Lou Brock, who became the game's all-time leader for stolen bases before being surpassed by Rickey Henderson in 1991. With a young "Lefty" named Steve Carlton and the great Bob Gibson taking their turns on the hill every four days, the Cardinals did not require much offense in order to win.

**Bob Gibson of the St. Louis Cardinals.**

## RECORD SETTING REDBIRD

Bob Gibson lost the first and last World Series games in which he appeared. In between, he recorded an unprecedented seven-straight complete-game victories. After winning Game 5 and Game 7 of the 1964 World Series, he was nearly untouchable in the 1967 Fall Classic. Bob suffered a broken leg that season when Roberto Clemente's line-shot caromed off his left hip. A nine-time Gold Glove Award winner, Gibby fielded the ball and threw the Hall-of-Fame Pirate out on the play! After recovering for eight weeks, he defeated the Boston Red Sox three-straight times in the World Series.

In the 1968 Fall Classic, Bob continued his record-setting ways. His 17 strikeouts in Game 1 broke a World Series mark set by Sandy Koufax five years earlier. In Game 4, Bob completed his seventh-consecutive World Series victory, and became the only pitcher to hit two home runs in post-season play. After losing Game 7, Bob Gibson would never return to the Fall Classic. He won a second NL Cy Young Award in 1970, and was elected to the Hall of Fame in 1981.

# Jim
# Palmer

Baltimore, Maryland, has been home to some of baseball's most historic events. It was the birthplace of Babe Ruth, who began his career as a pitcher for the minor-league Baltimore Orioles before being traded to the Boston Red Sox for cash. Prior to that, a pair of Oriole ballclubs migrated to New York City, where one became the Brooklyn Dodgers and the other the New York Yankees. It was only fair, therefore, that the "Big Apple" would produce a pitcher named Jim Palmer, who would help bring Baltimore's newest Orioles three World Championship seasons over the course of three decades.

James Alvin Palmer was the adopted son of Moe and Polly Wiesen. His youngest days were spent living in a luxury Manhattan apartment on Park Avenue, and on an estate in Westchester County, New York. This wealthy existence, in which the family's butler taught Jim to pitch, lasted nine years until Moe Wiesen suddenly passed away of a heart attack. Polly moved with Jim and his adopted older sister to Whittier, California, where she met and married actor Max Palmer. Jim's new father moved the family into a home in Beverly Hills, which was previously owned by James Cagney.

His new surroundings caused Jim to consider a movie career of his own, but he found baseball even more enticing. He was a third baseman for a Beverly Hills Little League team, until his natural pitching ability was discovered. Soon the family would be on the move again, landing in Scottsdale, Arizona, when Jim was 14. At Scottsdale High School, Jim was an All-State performer in baseball, football, and basketball. He was offered a basketball scholarship from UCLA (University of California in Los Angeles), where he could have joined a team that won three National Championships over the next four seasons. Saying later, "I guess I always wanted to be a ballplayer," Jim chose to pursue a career in baseball.

It didn't take long for Jim's aspirations to fulfill themselves. The summer following his high school graduation, he pitched for an amateur team in Winner, South Dakota. In August of that year, he was signed to a contract by the team that would employ him throughout his entire major league career! The Baltimore Orioles were building the nucleus for a pitching-arsenal that would carry them to six American League Pennants. In a 12 year span from 1969 to 1980, Baltimore's staff would account for six American League Cy Young Awards, including the three that went to Jim Palmer.

On April 17, 1965, Jim Palmer made his major league debut. The next season, he joined the starting-rotation, led the staff in wins, and pitched the first of his four pennant-clinching victories. Jim's

shutout over the Los Angeles Dodgers in the 1966 World Series came in the final game of Sandy Koufax's incredible career. The new Baltimore Orioles went on to win their first World Championship in a stunning four-game sweep.

Jim Palmer's long tenure with the Orioles witnessed the birth of a mighty dynasty, its collapse, and its resurgence. His career spanned the time when the legendary Brooks Robinson was Baltimore's third baseman, to the days when a shortstop named Cal Ripken, Jr. began his record-breaking streak of consecutive games played. Jim is the only pitcher who has won a World Series contest in three separate decades. It's one more significant note with regards to the history of baseball in Baltimore.

**PROFILE:**
Jim Palmer
Born: October 15, 1945
Height: 6' 3"
Weight: 196 pounds
Position: Pitcher
Throws: Right
Teams: Baltimore Orioles (1965-1967, 1969-1984)

## CHAMPIONSHIP
### SEASONS

*Jim Palmer*

1986
**World Series**
Baltimore Orioles (4) vs.
Los Angeles Dodgers (0)
1970
**World Series**
Baltimore Orioles (4) vs.
Cincinnati Reds (1)
1983
**World Series**
Baltimore Orioles (4) vs.
Philadelphia Phillies (1)

# BIRDS OF A FEATHER

The original Baltimore Orioles were a 19th Century National League dynasty. With Hall of Fame baseball legends John McGraw, Dan Brouthers, Hughie Jennings, Joe Kelley, Wilbert Robinson, Ned Hanlon, and "Wee" Willie Keeler, these birds won three-straight league pennants and two World Championships in the 1890s. Their "Hit 'em where they ain't" style gave rise to the baseball term "Baltimore chop," to describe a swinging bunt, which was both hard nosed and down right dirty. They merged with the Brooklyn Bridegrooms in 1900, to form a team that would eventually become known as the Dodgers.

John McGraw, meanwhile, would become the manager for the new American League's Baltimore Orioles in 1901. His bitter feud with the league's umpires caused him to jump to the New York Giants, taking Hall-of-Famers "Iron Man" Joe McGinnity and Roger Besnahan along with him. Deflated from the departure, this second flock of Orioles flew the coop as well. They became the New York Highlanders in 1903, who 23 years later, with help from a native of Baltimore named Babe Ruth, won their first of a record 23 World Championships as the Yankees.

# ST. LOUIS BROWNS

The current Baltimore Orioles were originally the St. Louis Browns, who aside from their American League Pennant in 1944, were consistently among the worst teams in baseball. They moved to Baltimore in 1954 and by the mid-1960s had built yet another Oriole dynasty. Paced by Hall-of-Famers Jim Palmer, Frank Robinson, and Brooks Robinson, they matched their 19th century ancestors with three-straight league pennants from 1969-1971.

## COME-BACKER

There are two kinds of come-backers in baseball. The first is a line-shot hit back at the pitcher, like the ones that broke Bob Gibson's leg, Dizzy Dean's toe, and Catfish Hunter's thumb. Then there are the players who return from injury to have successful seasons. Jim Palmer represents the second kind of come-backer.

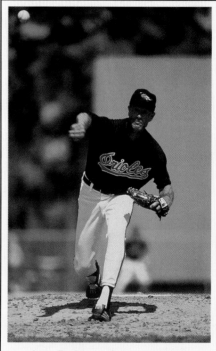

**Jim Palmer fires a pitch.**

After his success in the 1966 World Series, a sore back forced Jim to return to the minor-leagues. He returned in 1969 to lead the Orioles to their second American League Pennant. After four straight 20-win seasons, a tender elbow in 1974 caused him to suffer through the worst season of his career. In 1975, he began another four year streak of 20-win seasons and led the league in wins three-straight times.

Inspired by Nolan Ryan's longevity, Jim attempted one last comeback in 1991. He was 45 years old and had already been inducted into the Baseball Hall of Fame. When he was roughed-up in a couple of spring-training outings he decided to hang-up the spikes for good.

# Catfish Hunter

Down in Carolina where the dogwoods grow, a boy learns his lessons with a fishin' pole. Near the Blue Ridge Mountains where the Tar River's flow, came a fellow name of Catfish who was born to throw. He was a Hunter by name and a marksman by his trade. There's no tellin' how he spent all the money that he made. Hurlin' baseballs for a livin' he was the finest of his day. He could have played longer but he didn't want to stay. From California to New York many batters they fell under, the spellbinding ways of Mr. Catfish Hunter!

His name is James Augustus, but the townsfolk call him Jimmy. He received his nickname "Catfish" from the owner of the Athletics, Charles O. Finley. "We'll tell the folks you was at the fishin' hole when they found you sleeping by the stream with a Catfish on your pole!" Finley told Hunter. And so a legendary tale was born, though Jim's mother didn't like it.

But when Catfish threw, the scorn he drew came from batters who could not strike it.

Jim "Catfish" Hunter was the youngest of Millie and Abbott Hunter's eight children. He grew up on his daddy's farm near Hertford, North Carolina. "We didn't have much money, but we always had baseball," brother Pete remembers. "We could get a game goin' just in the family. We'd play in the cow pastures and yards. When it rained, we'd go in the barn, break up corncobs and hit them with a stick."

At Perquimans High School, Jim was a linebacker on the football team and a shortstop in baseball. He was also an outstanding pitcher who had thrown five no-hit ballgames,

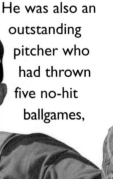

when an accidental shooting nearly ended his Hall of Fame career before it began. On a Thanksgiving Day duck hunting trip, Pete's shotgun discharged without warning. The ensuing blast nearly obliterated his brother's right foot. Doctors surgically removed as many pellets as they could reach and amputated what was left of Jim's shattered little toe.

Suddenly, many of the major league scouts who had been following Jim's development quit calling. Still numb from anesthesia and barely able to walk, Jim began working to recover his pitching-motion. Meanwhile, Clyde Kluttz a scout for the Kansas City Athletics had not lost interest. "In his senior year of high school, he wasn't able to push-off the mound, but he still had the smooth delivery," Kluttz reported. The Athletics' eccentric owner, Charles O. Finley, decided to take a chance. He signed Jim to a contract and sent him to Minnesota's Mayo Clinic for a second operation. There they removed another 27 pellets from his damaged foot.

Catfish Hunter never spent a day in the minor leagues. His career began with the Kansas City Athletics in 1965, and the next season he was named to his first American League All-Star team. When the A's moved to Oakland, California, in 1968, Catfish fired the league's first perfect game in over 40 years! In 1974, he was the Cy Young Award winner, as Oakland completed their third-consecutive World Championship season.

The New York Yankees and their owner George Steinbrenner won a free-agent bidding-war over Catfish in 1975, making him the richest player in the game. In return, Catfish helped the Yankees to three-straight American League Pennants and another pair of World Championship seasons. When his contract was up, Catfish Hunter retired at the age of 33. He returned to life on a North Carolina farm, where he undoubtedly spends his well-earned free-time down by the fishin' hole!

**PROFILE:**
Catfish Hunter
Born: April 8, 1946
Height: 6'
Weight: 195 pounds
Position: Pitcher
Throws: Right
Teams: Kansas City Athletics (1965-1967), Oakland Athletics (1968-1974), New York Yankees (1975-1979)

## CHAMPIONSHIP

### SEASONS

*1972*

**World Series**
Oakland Athletics (4) vs.
Cincinnati Reds (3)

*1973*

**World Series**
Oakland Athletics (4) vs.
New York Mets (3)

*1974*

**World Series**
Oakland Athletics (4) vs.
Los Angeles Dodgers (1)

*1977*

**World Series**
New York Yankees (4) vs.
Los Angeles Dodgers (2)

*1978*

**World Series**
New York Yankees (4) vs.
Los Angeles Dodgers (2)

# PERFECTION

No-hit ballgames are a rarity in baseball. Perfection is almost unheard of. There have been only 13 perfect pitching performances in the entire history of Major League Baseball. The most recent came from Dennis Martinez, who sent 27 straight Dodger batters to the bench on July 28, 1991, while pitching for the Montreal Expos. Len Barker, Mike Witt, and Tom Browning all turned the trick in the 1980s, while no pitcher was perfect in the previous decade.

The first perfect game was thrown by Lee Richmond in 1880, who was the only player to do it prior to the legalization of the overhand pitch. Cy Young was the first to do it after 1900, followed by Addie Joss in 1908. The next perfect performance came in 1917, in a game involving—who else—Babe Ruth. After disputing a walk call to the lead-off batter in the first inning, Babe was ejected from the game for slugging the umpire. Ernie Shore entered the game in relief, picked-off the baserunner, and sent the next 26 Washington Senators down in order.

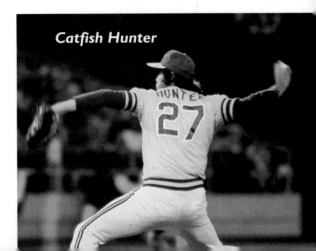

*Catfish Hunter*

# PERFECT GEM

Charlie Robertson's perfect-gem in 1922 was followed by more than three decades of less than perfect mound-work. The streak was broken in 1956, when Don Larsen of the New York Yankees blanked the Brooklyn Dodgers in the only perfect World Series performance. Sandy Koufax and Jim Bunning each had perfect National League outings in the 1960s, while Harvey Haddix threw 12 perfect innings for the Pittsburgh Pirates in 1959, only to lose to the Milwaukee Braves 0-1 in the 13th!

Catfish Hunter's hitless, errorless, and walk-free game came on May 8, 1968, against the Minnesota Twins. He threw 107 pitches, striking-out 11 batters, and not a single difficult defensive play was needed. Along with his eight All-Star selections, six American League Pennants, and five World Championship seasons, Catfish had all the credentials necessary to reach baseball immortality. Commissioner Peter Ueberroth observed, "Catfish Hunter had the distinction of playing for both Charlie Finley and George Steinbrenner, which [on its own] is enough to put a player in the Hall of Fame!"

*Catfish Hunter pitching
for the Oakland A's.*

# Nolan Ryan

Texas has long been known for its sweltering heat. In 1965, the city of Houston, Texas, opened baseball's first domed stadium in an attempt to find a cooler environment in which to play the game. The next season, a future Houston Astro and native Texan began heating up Major League Baseball with a fastball clocked at over 100 miles per hour! His name was Nolan Ryan, and he became baseball's all-time strikeout king.

Nolan Ryan played 27 seasons in the major leagues, eventually striking out players who weren't even born when his career began. When he broke Walter Johnson's 56-year-old record for career strikeouts in 1983, he still had 10 seasons left in which to accumulate his own untouchable total of 5,714. You might say, Nolan just kept throwing and throwing and throwing. He broke Sandy Koufax's record for no-hit ballgames on September 26, 1981, with his fifth such performance. Then in 1990, Nolan became the oldest player to accomplish the feat, before breaking his own record with a seventh no-hitter at the age of 44.

In his career with the New York Mets, California Angels, Houston Astros, and Texas Rangers, Nolan set or tied over 50 separate records for strikeouts, as well as no-hit and low-hit ballgames. He is the modern-day record holder for strikeouts in a season with 383. He is one of only six players who have ever averaged more than 10 strikeouts per game over an entire season, an achievement he accomplished a record eight times! Yet, with all of his success he won only one World Championship, and that season was considered to be a Miracle!

Lynn Nolan Ryan, Jr. was the youngest of six children in his family. He was born in Refugio, Texas, and grew up near the town of Alvin, Texas. His father simultaneously worked for the American Oil Company and as a distributor of a Houston newspaper. His mother stayed home to take care of the family, raising her children with the hard-working conservative values that would become the essence of Nolan's success. He also learned the value of a dollar, getting up before dawn each day to help his father deliver the daily news.

Baseball was as important to Nolan's early development as any other single activity. "When I was eight years old I knew I could throw the ball past batters," he'd later say. Along with his neighbor-hood friends, he would spend entire days under the blistering Texas sky, learning the game that would make him famous. Before long, he would develop a fastball that had the ability of striking fear into the hearts of the opposition.

At Alvin High School, Nolan was an All-State performer, earned the Outstanding Athlete Award, and met the girl he would eventually marry. "I was wild in those days," he recalled. "And I didn't have a curve-ball because nobody in town knew how to throw one." In one outing, he cracked the batting-helmet of the first player he faced,

broke the arm of the second, and wound-up recording 19-of-21 outs (in the seven inning contest)—on strikeouts!

It is hard to imagine any pitcher ever dethroning the reigning strikeout king of Major League Baseball. Steve Carlton currently ranks second on the list after finishing his own outstanding career more than 1,500 strikeouts short of Nolan's incredible total. From the bright lights of New York City, where he won his only World Championship, to the sweltering heat of Texas, nothing has ever out-matched the scorching fastball of Nolan Ryan.

**PROFILE:**
Nolan Ryan
Born: January 31, 1947
Height: 6' 2"
Weight: 195 pounds
Position: Pitcher
Throws: Right
Teams: New York Mets (1966, 1968-71), California Angels (1972-1979), Houston Astros (1980-1988), Texas Rangers (1989-1993)

**33**

## CHAMPIONSHIP

### SEASONS

**Nolan Ryan with the Texas Rangers.**

1969

**World Series**
New York Mets (4) vs.
Baltimore Orioles (1)

# MIRACLE METS

The New York Mets and Houston Colt .45s (the original Astros) joined the National League through expansion in 1962. Throughout their first seven seasons, the two teams battled it out for last-place in the league, with the "Amazin' Mets" generally earning the dubious honor. In 1968, the Mets and Astros played 23 innings of a scoreless tie, before Houston finally pushed across the winning-run with a ground-ball that rolled through the legs of New York's shortstop!

The following season the Mets made a miraculous turn-around. New York's Tom Seaver took the first of his three Cy Young Awards in 1969, as the team won 22 of their final 27 games to catch the Chicago Cubs and advance to the first National League Championship Series. There, New York met the Atlanta Braves in a best-of-five-game matchup. The 22 year old Nolan Ryan pitched seven innings of relief in Game 3 to earn a pennant-clinching victory. The Mets completed their "Miracle" season by defeating the powerful Baltimore Orioles in the World Series!

**Nolan checks the catcher's signs.**

# TEXAS HEAT

Among the few major league strikeout records not held by Nolan Ryan is the mark for a single-game performance. That record is held by fellow Texan, Roger Clemens. "The Rocket" struck out 20 batters in a game twice while pitching for the Boston Red Sox.

The National League record of 19 strikeouts in a game is shared by Tom Seaver and Steve Carlton. Nolan Ryan reached that plateau four times (including three 19 strikeout performances in 1974), while pitching for the American League's California Angels.

*Nolan—bringing on the heat.*

# *R*YAN EXPRESS

Nolan Ryan's longevity as a big league pitcher is attributable to his rigorous workout schedule. While his incredible fastball was partially an in-born ability, he developed and maintained it through a habit of daily exercise. At the age of 46, he was still among the hardest throwing pitchers in the game, reaching speeds of more than 90 mph. Immediately after completing his incredible seventh no-hitter, the course of the "Ryan Express" led directly to the training room, where he could be found riding the Lifecycle!

# Fernando Valenzuela

Baseball is an international endeavor. While it is known as America's national pastime, it is among the most popular sports in several countries around the World. In Japan, baseball has surpassed the native sport of sumo as the nation's favorite pastime activity. Long before the Montreal Expos and Toronto Blue Jays joined Major League Baseball, it was the summertime game of choice in the hockey-crazed country of Canada.

South of the border, baseball is played during America's winter-months. Places such as the Dominican Republic, Cuba, Puerto Rico, Nicaragua, and Mexico have been producing some of the game's finest talent for over 100 years. Among the legions of stars who have traveled north to display their talent in the big leagues is a pitcher the Mexican people nicknamed "Zurdo (Lefty) Fernando!"

In 1981, Fernando Valenzuela became the first player in major league history to win the Rookie of the Year and Cy Young Awards in the same season. To top it off, he also led the Los Angeles Dodgers to that season's World Championship. Latin-Americans living in the area of Los Angeles had a new baseball hero. Fans flocked to Dodger Stadium in ever increasing numbers each time Fernando was scheduled to take the mound. The entire baseball world was swept into a sensation that became commonly known as Fernando-mania!

Fernando Anguamea Valenzuela was born in the state of Sonora, Mexico. He was the youngest of Avelino and Maria Hermengilda Valenzuela's 12 children. Avelino was a farmer in the village of Etchohuaquila, Sonora. The family's ancestry is Taracahitian Indian, or Mayo as the Taracahitian people of Sonora, Mexico call themselves. Fernando has six older brothers, most of whom went to work on farms and ranches near their home. "My brother Rafeal was the first one who told me I could play baseball professionally," Fernando recalls. "He had played pro ball himself, so he knew. He gave me confidence."

At the age of 15, Fernando was chosen to pitch for the Navojoa area all-star team. They became the Sonora State Champions, with Fernando tossing three victories in the tournament's final rounds. He was named the MVP of the championship series, and selected to play for the Sonora State all-star team in the national competition at Baja, California. After that, he began a professional career, which eventually led him to the Yucatan Lions of the Mexican League.

Meanwhile, Fernando was beginning to draw attention of major league scouts from the United States. Four months before he turned 19, Fernando signed a contract with the Los Angeles Dodgers. He completed the 1979 season in the California League, where in three starting assignments he allowed fewer than two runs per game. After the season, he traveled to an Arizona Instructional League where he developed his most devastating delivery. The "screw-ball" would become Fernando's signature pitch, and by the end of the next season he would use it to secure his place on the Dodgers' major league roster.

In the 1980s, Fernando Valenzuela became the latest in a long line of Latin-American pitchers who have gone on to greatness in Major League Baseball. After a decade of dominance, his tired arm caused him to return to his native land, where he began a comeback in the Mexican League. He returned to America one year later, and in 1996 he pitched for the San Diego Padres in the first Major League Baseball game played south of the border.

**PROFILE:**
Fernando Valenzuela
Born: November 1, 1960
Height: 5' 11"
Weight: 195 pounds
Position: Pitcher
Throws: Left
Teams: Los Angeles Dodgers (1980-1990), California Angels (1991), Baltimore Orioles (1993), Philadelphia Phillies (1994), San Diego Padres (1995- )

*Fernando winds up.*

1981
**World Series**
Los Angeles Dodgers (4)
vs. New York Yankees (2)

1988
**World Series**
Los Angeles Dodgers (4)
vs. Oakland Athletics (1)

# SOUTH OF THE BORDER

Baseball's popularity was spread to areas south of the United States in the nineteenth century. Since then, several Latin-American players have had an impact on the game. Prior to 1947, most of these players were barred from major league competition by the same agreement that prevented people of African descent from playing in the majors. The exceptions were those players whose skin color was actually light enough to pass Major League Baseball's ridiculous requirements.

Among the light-skinned Latinos who preceded Jackie Robinson to the major leagues was a Cuban-born pitching star named Adolpho Luque. "The Pride of Havana" played 20 seasons in the National League. He recorded 27 wins in 1923, with a 1.93 ERA to lead the Senior Circuit in both categories. Dolph also won Game 5 of the 1933 World Series to seal the World Championship for the New York Giants.

Juan Marichal was the staff-ace of the San Francisco Giants in the 1960s. "Manito" was from Laguna Verde, in the Dominican Republic. He was a nine-time All-Star in a Hall-of-Fame career, which included 243 wins. Marichal's record for Latin-American pitchers will most likely be surpassed by Dennis Martinez who entered the 1997 season with 240 wins. "El Presidente" is from Granada, Nicaragua.

# SINCE SANDY

Fernando Valenzuela was selected for the All-Star Game six-straight times in the 1980s. He was baseball's most durable starting pitcher during that span, winning more games than any other National Leaguer. His 20 complete games in 1986 were the most by a Dodger hurler since Sandy Koufax went the route 27 times 20 years earlier. In 1990, Fernando joined Sandy in the club of Dodger pitchers who have thrown no-hitters.

## FERNANDO-MANIA

Fernado Valenzuela became a popular sensation almost immediately after his major league debut in 1980. His characteristic wind-up, in which he looks skyward before delivering the ball, combined with his backwards curve, youthful 20 year old looks, and Mexican descent gave fans plenty to stir about. Opposing batters, meanwhile, had a difficult time adjusting to the rookie southpaw. He won his first eight starting assignments, set a rookie record with eight shutouts, and led the National League in shutouts, strikeouts, complete-games and innings-pitched in 1981.

*Fernando (left) in action with the Phillies and the Dodgers (right).*

# Greg
# Maddux

Instinct is the ability to sense and react on a given set of circumstances. In baseball, the batter must react to a pitch traveling at high velocity, while the pitcher uses their instincts to understand the given situation and read the batter's mind. Even if they do know what the batter is thinking, a pitcher must still have the mechanical ability to control where the ball is going to end up. An instinctive pitcher with control can have a devastating effect on an offense. Ask any batter who has ever faced Greg Maddux.

Keeping the offense off balance is the "Mad Dog's" specialty. He does not possess an overwhelming fastball or any single pitch more dominant than another. He simply knows what the batter wants, and he doesn't give it to them. "The best way I can describe it," said Greg's pitching coach Leo Mazzone, "is that he can throw you a strike and still not give you anything good to hit."

In an era when offenses are scoring more runs than ever before, Greg Maddux has statistics comparable to pitching greats of the "dead-ball" era. He became the only player since the introduction of the Cy Young Award in 1956, to win the honor in four consecutive seasons. He is already a master of his craft, and he is intent on improving.

Gregory Alan Maddux was born in San Angelo, Texas. His father David Maddux was in the United States Air Force before retiring and moving his family to Las Vegas, Nevada. There, David became a card dealer for a casino while his sons Michael and Greg were kings of the local baseball diamonds.

Mike Maddux is five years older than Greg, and both would go on to careers as major league pitchers. At Valley High School in Las Vegas, Greg was an All-State performer in his junior and senior seasons. Immediately after his graduation he was drafted by the Chicago Cubs. Two years later, he would face Mike in Major League Baseball's first match-up to feature a pair of rookies who were also brothers. Greg recorded the second victory of what was about to become a historic career.

In his seven seasons with the Cubs, Greg developed the confidence necessary to throw any one of his pitches anytime. He also became a defensive specialist, winning the first of six consecutive Gold Glove Awards at the center of the diamond, in 1991. The next season he led the National League in victories with an impressive 2.18 ERA, to pick up the first of four-straight Cy Young Awards. After the 1992 season, he signed as a free-agent with the Atlanta Braves.

Greg won a National League East Division Title with the Chicago Cubs in 1989. Seeing the potential of Atlanta's "Young Guns" pitching-staff he decided to join them. Once again his instincts proved correct. In 1995, the Braves became World Champions. That year, Greg Maddux became the first pitcher since the great Walter Johnson to have an earned run average below 1.80 in two-consecutive seasons.

The center of a diamond is a special place. The game of baseball revolves around it. To succeed there, a player must have great skill and above all the instinct of a *Champion!*

**_PROFILE_:**
Greg Maddux
Born: April 14, 1966
Height: 6'
Weight: 150 pounds
Position: Pitcher
Throws: Right
Teams: Chicago Cubs (1986-1992),
Atlanta Braves (1993- )

## CHAMPIONSHIP

### SEASONS

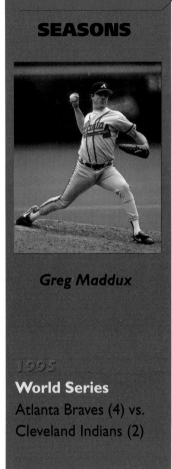

*Greg Maddux*

1995
**World Series**
Atlanta Braves (4) vs.
Cleveland Indians (2)

# YOUNG GUNS

In 1993, Greg Maddux joined a rotation that already included a pair of the National League's finest pitchers. Together Atlanta's "Young Guns" have accounted for six-consecutive Cy Young Awards. Prior to Greg's arrival, the Braves were carried to the 1991 National League Pennant by Tom Glavine's award winning season. Tom would also be named the MVP of the 1995 Fall Classic. In 1996, the Atlanta Braves won their fourth pennant of the decade, as John Smoltz followed Greg's record-setting string of Cy Young Awards with a league-leading performance of his own.

*Greg Maddux winds up.*

# WHO'S THE FINEST OF THEM ALL?

The Cy Young Award was introduced in 1956 to honor each season's finest pitcher. Don Newcombe of the Brooklyn Dodgers was the first recipient. In 1965 and 1966, Sandy Koufax became the only player other than Greg Maddux to win the award in consecutive seasons. Since 1967, one pitcher from each league has been chosen to receive the honor.

Steve Carlton is the only player other than Greg Maddux who has won four Cy Young Awards. Tom Seaver, Jim Palmer, Roger Clemens, and Sandy Koufax were all named to the honor three times.

It is estimated that Cy Young himself would have won six Cy Young Awards, had there been such an honor when he played. Walter "Big Train" Johnson and Christy Mathewson may have taken home as many as seven apiece! Walter's 417 career wins ranks second to Cy's 511

*Greg Maddux pitching for the Braves.*

on baseball's all-time leader board. Greg Maddux's consistency as the National League's most dominant pitcher is reminiscent of the great pitchers from baseball's "Dead Ball" Era!

*Greg Maddux throwing heat.*

**43**

# Glossary

**All-American:** A person chosen as the best amateur athlete at his position.

**All-Star:** A player who is voted by fans as the best player at his position in a given year. American and National League All-Stars have been facing off each summer since 1933 in the All-Star Game.

**American League (AL):** An association of baseball teams that make-up one half of the Major Leagues.

**American League Championship Series (ALCS):** A best of seven game playoff with the winner going to the World Series to face the National League Champions.

**Batting Average:** A baseball statistic calculated by dividing a batters hits by the number of times at bat.

**Contract:** A written agreement players sign when they are hired by a professional team.

**Defense:** The part of a team attempting to prevent the opposition from scoring.

**Draft:** A system in which new players are distributed to professional sports teams.

**Earned Run Average (ERA):** A baseball statistic that calculates the average number of runs a pitcher gives up per nine innings of work.

**Freshman:** A student in the first year of a U.S. high school or college.

**Hall of Fame:** A memorial for the greatest players of all time located in Cooperstown, New York.

**Home Run (HR):** A play in baseball where a batter hits the ball over the outfield fence scoring everyone on base as well as himself.

**Junior:** A student in the third year of a U.S. high school or college.

**Major Leagues:** The highest ranking associations of professional baseball teams in the world, currently consisting of the American and National Baseball Leagues.

**Minor leagues:** A system of professional baseball leagues at levels below Major League Baseball.

**National League (NL):** An association of baseball teams formed in 1876 that make-up one half of the Major Leagues.

**National League Championship Series (NLCS):** A best of seven game playoff with the winner going to the World Series to face the American League Champions.

**Pennant:** A flag that symbolizes the championship of a professional baseball league.

**Pitcher:** The player on a baseball team who throws the ball for the batter to hit. He stands on a mound and pitches the ball toward the strike zone area above the plate.

**Plate:** The place on a baseball field where a player stands to bat. It is used to determine the width of the strike zone. Forming the point of the diamond shaped field, it is the final goal a baserunner must reach to score a run.

**Professional:** A person who is paid for his work.

**RBI:** A baseball statistic standing for *runs batted in.* A player receives an RBI for each run that scores on his hit.

**Rookie:** A first-year player, especially in a professional sport.

**Senior:** A student in the fourth year of a U.S. high school or college.

**Sophomore:** A student in the second year of a U.S. high school or college.

**Stolen Base:** A play in baseball when a baserunner advances to the next base while the pitcher is delivering his pitch.

**Strike Out:** A play in baseball when a batter is called out for failing to put the ball in play after the pitcher has delivered three strikes.

**Triple Crown:** A rare accomplishment when a single player finishes a season leading his league in batting average, home runs and RBIs. A pitcher can win a Triple Crown by leading his league in wins, ERA, and strike outs.

**Varsity:** The principal team representing a university, college, or school in sports, games, or other competitions.

**Veteran:** A player with more than one year of professional experience.

**Walk:** A play in baseball when a batter receives four pitches out of the strike zone and is allowed to go to first base, (Base on Balls).

**World Series:** The championship of Major League Baseball played since 1903, between the pennant winners from the American and National leagues.

# Index